THE HOBBIT™

THE BATTLE OF THE FIVE ARMIES

VISUAL COMPANION

JUDE FISHER

HarperCollins*Publishers*

CONTENTS

INTRODUCTION

BY SIR IAN McKELLEN

London 2014.

All of us who have read *The Hobbit* have imagined Middle-earth for ourselves, aided in some editions of the book, by the matchless illustrations of John Howe and Alan Lee. These two artists, thanks to Peter Jackson's good taste and common sense, have together made real on the screen what Tolkien described on the page. So now we all share their vision.

The minute I landed in New Zealand in 2000, to film *The Lord of the Rings*, I felt at home in the varying landscapes, where hobbits, wizards and orcs could well inhabit. It was as if the mountains and plains, the heathland and forests, had been waiting, in sunshine or snow, as the perfect background for their story.

Even so, the wait was inevitable, because even New Zealand's landscapes were not enough to re-create a believable background for the exploits of Middle-earth's inhabitants. I mean, how do you shrink normal-sized actors into hobbits? How does the eagle Gwahir fly? or Smaug the dragon for that matter? The magic of modern technology had to be invented to bring them all to cinematic life.

WETA workshops designs, models and computers were indispensible. Although the actors were filmed outdoors on location across New Zealand, we were more frequently in the custom-built studios at Miramar, close by the capital Wellington. One day, perhaps, there will be a permanent museum to explain how it was achieved. If so, I'll be happy to loan Gandalf's sword and pointy blue-grey hat, which I was given when we finally finished filming the *The Hobbit* trilogy.

Technology is one thing: but it would be nothing, without the spirit and hard work of the hundreds of Kiwis and non-Kiwis whose names roll up the screen at the end of each film. Together we lived the adventure, transforming fiction into apparent fact. It has been privilege to be a part of it all.

By the time *The Hobbit: The Battle of the Five Armies* was underway, we knew that you were with us. Peter Jackson, perhaps Tolkien's most dedicated supporter, often told us we were working for the multitudinous fans of the previous five films, waiting across the world for the story to be completed. Now, aided by this handsome book, you can see for yourselves what the film-makers imagined.

THE LONELY MOUNTAIN

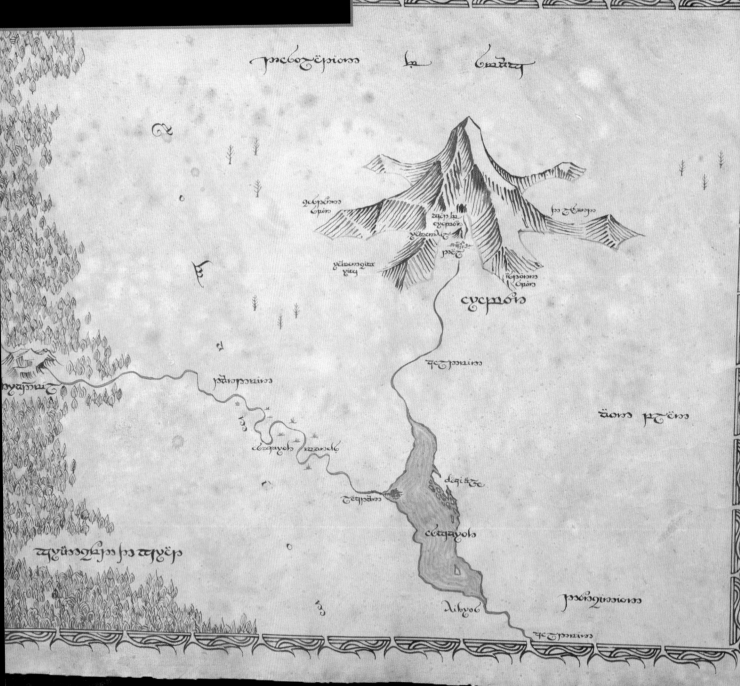

THE LONELY MOUNTAIN

THE LIZARD RIDGE

ERN SPUR

THRUSHTONE SHELF

BIRDFLIGHT RIDGE

RAVENWING RIDGE

RAZORBACK RIDGE

GATES OF EREBOR

RAVENHILL

THE CITY OF DALE

EASTERN SPUR

ESGAROTH CAUSEWAY

RUNNING PLATEAU

IRON PLATEAU

SOUTHEAST KNOLL

BIRDSEYE TOR

THE RIVER RUNNING

THE

DESOLATION

OF

SMAUG

THE JOURNEY CONTINUES

The hobbit Bilbo Baggins has been singled out by the wizard Gandalf to become a member of the Company of Thorin Oakenshield. The Company consists of thirteen Dwarves – Thorin and his nephews, Kili and Fili, trusted counsellor Balin and his warlike brother Dwalin, gentlemanly Dori and his younger brothers Nori and Ori, the Company's herb-expert Oin and his brother Gloin, and from the Blue Mountains, Bofur and his cousins, the war-damaged Bifur and the Company's cook, the impressively rotund Bombur.

Thorin is the rightful King Under the Mountain, heir to the ancient dwarven realm of Erebor, known to Men as the Lonely Mountain. He carries a map drawn by his grandfather Thrór, showing a secret door carved into the rock, and a key to unlock it. For, hidden from sight inside the roots of the mountain, there lie cavernous chambers, towering halls and a vast treasure amassed over generations by gold-loving Dwarves. But during the time of Thrór's reign, drawn by the presence of so much gold, the dragon Smaug attacked Erebor and drove the Dwarves out, condemning the survivors of its murderous attack to a life of nomadic poverty.

Bilbo has been recruited to act as the Company's burglar: to slip unnoticed into the mountain and there find the Arkenstone, a crucial symbol of power, which will aid the Dwarves in taking back their lost homeland. It is said that the scent of hobbits is unknown to dragons, and therefore Bilbo is best suited for the job. It is clearly a dangerous mission, not much to the taste of any respectable hobbit. But Bilbo is no ordinary hobbit…

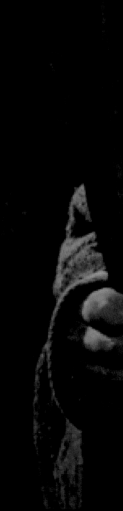

Travelling from the safe haven of the Shire out into the Wild, the Company was captured by three trolls, although Bilbo's quick-thinking helped to save them from becoming tasty snacks, delaying their despatch until Gandalf was able to expose the trolls to the rays of the rising sun, which turned the three to stone.

The Company encountered Gandalf's friend and fellow wizard, Radagast the Brown. A remarkable character who lives on the edge of what was once called the Greenwood, he has strong links to the wildlife, the fauna and natural balance of Middle-earth and has noticed how the woods are being corrupted by dark magic leaking out of the ancient fortress at Dol Guldur, where a sorcerer known as the Necromancer appears to have taken up residence.

Pursued by Orcs and Wargs, the Company managed to find their way through a stone passage to Rivendell, the Last Homely House in the West, a refuge for Elves ruled over by the Lord Elrond. In Rivendell, by the light of the moon, Elrond was able to decipher the 'moon runes' on the map Thorin carries, in which a secret inscription had been made advising anyone wishing to enter Erebor to 'Stand by the grey stone when the thrush knocks and the setting sun with the last of Durin's Day will shine upon the keyhole'.

But Lord Elrond did not approve
of the Company's mission, and so
Bilbo and the Dwarves slipped
away while Elrond, Gandalf, the White
Wizard Saruman and Galadriel, the
White Lady of Lórien, held a council to
discuss the creeping evil that threatens
Middle-earth. While investigating Dol
Guldur, Radagast had been attacked by a
wraithlike being wielding a weapon that
was buried with an ancient enemy in a deep
mountain tomb. Surviving the encoun-
ter, he had passed this morgul-blade to
Gandalf to show to the Council as proof of
the resurrection of evil. But Saruman dis-
counted it out of hand, regarding Radagast
as a fool. Others, being more wary, were
less dismissive.

The Company trekked through pre-
cipitous passes in the neighbouring Misty
Mountains on their way east, surviving a

colossal battle between boulder-hurling stone giants, storms and rockfall, but then falling prey to the goblins that infest the mountains: diseased, monstrous creatures led by the Great Goblin.

While his fellows were taken captive, Bilbo fell into the roots of the mountains where he came upon a disturbing creature called Gollum and there, in a riddle contest, came away with a magical golden ring which has the power to make him invisible.

The arrival of Gandalf enabled the Company to fight their way out of Goblin-town, only to be ambushed by the monstrous albino Orc, Azog, and his hunting party. Climbing trees to evade the snapping jaws of the Wargs, the Company was saved by the Eagles, who swooped down and carried them all off to the great rock known as the Carrock, on the edge of the territory of a giant of a man called Beorn.

Beorn is a skin-changer with the terrifying ability to transform himself into a huge bear and is a dangerous ally: for when he is in his bear-form he seems unable to distinguish friend from foe. From Beorn's house, the Company travelled east to the eaves of the great forest now known as Mirkwood. There, at the Forest Gate, Gandalf parted from them, leaving them with strict instructions to stay on the path, promising to rendezvous at the Overlook in the foothills of the Lonely Mountain.

Upon the request of the Lady Galadriel, Gandalf set off to investigate the High Fells, where once nine enemies of Middle-earth were entombed. There, he met with Radagast the Brown: together they discovered that the tombs had been broken open. For this was where the morgul-blade had been buried, the tombs sealed with magic, and only one possesses a magic powerful enough to have broken the spell. Sending Radagast back to report this dire news, Gandalf proceeded to Dol Guldur: a perilous mission indeed.

Meanwhile, the Company entered the forest, finding it dark and grim, filled with poisonous fungi and strange creatures. They were attacked by gigantic spiders, who cocooned them in their sticky webs and hung them from high branches to eat at their leisure. All that is, but Bilbo who armed with the Elven blade taken from the trolls' hoard, heroically rescued his companions. And so, Bilbo's sword earned a name, as all great weapons should: Sting.

But the dangers were not over: for the spiders were legion and although the Company battled hard they would surely have been overwhelmed if not for the intervention of a cadre of Woodland Elves led by their captain: a female warrior called Tauriel, and the son of King Thranduil, Legolas Greenleaf. Thinking them spies, they took the Dwarves captive and imprisoned them in the dungeons of the Elvenking's palace. There Thorin, rightful King Under the Mountain, and Thranduil of the Woodland Realm confronted one another once more and the festering resentment between Dwarves and the Elves flared once again into enmity.

The Company might well have been left to rot in the Elvenking's dungeons were it not for the ingenuity of Bilbo Baggins, who devised a brilliant plan to escape the palace. Down through the hatches into the river the Dwarves crashed, each in his own barrel, until they came to the closed sluice-gate, where the terrible Azog the Defiler and his Orcs and Wargs caught up with them.

In the skirmish that ensued, Kili was badly injured. But the Company found assistance in an unexpected aid: Tauriel, head of the king's guard, gave chase in an attempt to recapture the prisoners (although she had also formed a tenderness for the handsome young Dwarf Kili). Encountering a band of Orcs, the Elves battled their enemies in a spectacular fight, and the Company managed to continue downriver in their barrels to the apparent safety of Lake-town, where they were aided by a bargeman called Bard and smuggled into his house.

Lake-town had once been prosperous and thriving, but trade fell away as a result of the danger of the dragon in the nearby mountain and the simmering tensions between the peoples in the area. Now it is seedy and rundown, operating under the corrupt regime of the Master, aided by his lickspittle sidekick, Alfrid. Its people are poor, barely scraping a living tension and danger grips the town.

Bard and his family – daughters Sigrid and Tilda, and son Bain – are the last scions of the noble house of Girion, Lord of Dale, who fell defending his city from the dragon. Firing arrow after arrow at the monster, he failed to do any more than dislodge a single scale. Bard has lived in the shadow of his ancestor's failure: he can imagine nothing worse than to have the dragon awakened once more.

But Thorin has come too far on his quest to turn back now. Appealing to the greed of men, and the venality of the Master in particular, he promised wealth would once more flow into Lake-town if his mountain kingdom was restored. And so, the Master reprovisioned the Company and Bard was thrown into gaol as a troublemaker. However, Kili's wound had festered so he, his brother Fili and Bofur were left behind while the rest of the Company continued to the mountain in order to reach the secret door before Durin's Day.

Meanwhile, Gandalf made his way to Dol Guldur to confirm his suspicions about the true identity of the evil presence there. Penetrating the spell of concealment that lay upon the ruined fortress, he discovered that an army of fell creatures was being gathered there and the enemy within was revealed in all its awful glory. Whilst the Necromancer had not yet fully recovered its strength or its corporeal power, Gandalf was still defeated and held prisoner in that grim place.

And so it was that Gandalf was not present at the Overlook when Thorin and Company reached it and they continued up the Mountain on Durin's Day without him. By the light of the moon they found the keyhole and Thorin once more entered his kingdom. Now Bilbo's role as burglar came to the fore. He entered the treasure hall which was now the dragon's lair: and there found the monster, Smaug the Magnificent, buried beneath the gold and jewels that generations of Dwarves had gathered with such avarice and pride...

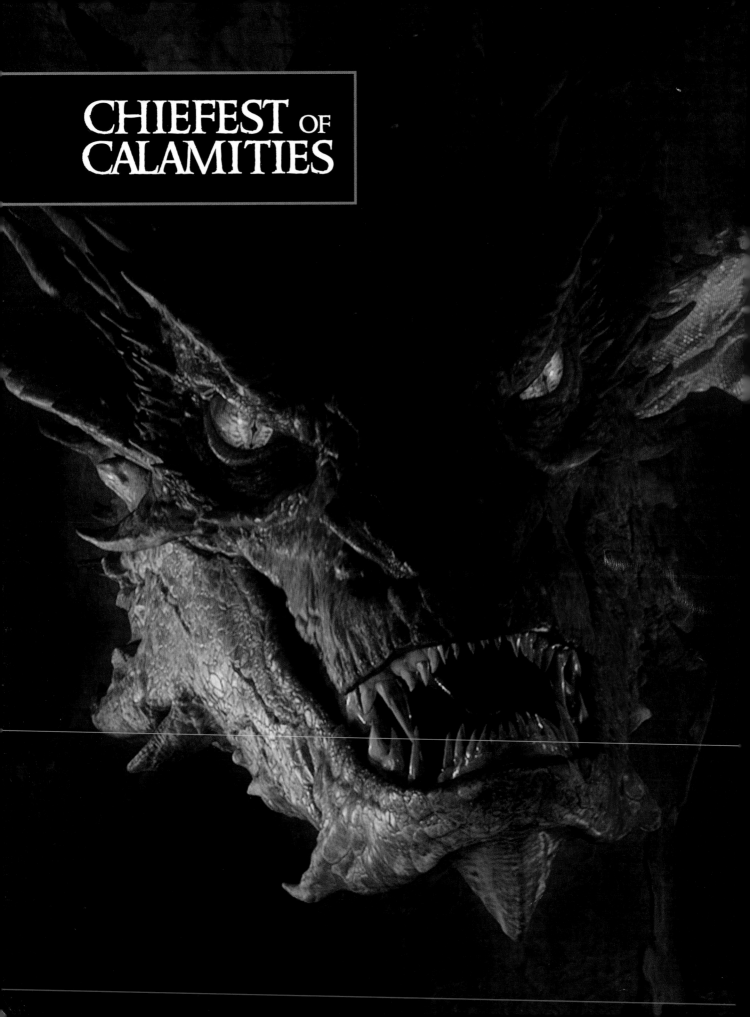

CHIEFEST OF CALAMITIES

Dragons love gold, more than they love anything in the world, including their young: for they are by nature solitary creatures that prefer the inanimate to the living. Some might say dragons love gold even more than they love their own lives: for what sort of a life is it to spend the better part of two hundred years inside a dark mountain, coiled around a heap of cold metal that can neither be eaten or used in any practical way. And yet, this is all that Smaug, that vast fire-drake from the north, has done these many years.

Smaug has spent years pressing his belly-scales against the cold metal, burrowing into the heap of jewels and goblets and plate and coins, dreaming the cold, acquisitive dreams of dragons, and woe betide anyone who disturbs him.

Dragons are ancient, vast, powerful and well-nigh immortal creatures. They are wily, intelligent and mighty. It is said that the scream of a dragon can deafen men, split stone, fell trees. And dragon-fire, unleashed with full-throated fury from the furnace of a fire-drake's breast is the most corrosive, destructive substance known to Middle-earth: even an elvenking has little defence against it. Thranduil himself has suffered the scars from that searing heat.

Smaug the Magnificent, lured down into the Gallery of Kings by Thorin and his Company, does not appreciate being

I WILL SHOW YOU REVENGE! I AM FIRE! I AM DEATH!

showered in gold that has been molten in the forges of the Dwarves of Erebor. In fact, it seems to have infuriated him beyond measure.

Charging out of the mountain like a thunderbolt, shedding liquid gold from his wings, Smaug heads for the nearby settlement of Lake-town with murder in his heart.

BARD & THE BLACK ARROW

Bard works as a bargeman in Lake-town: a hard, menial job, but one he is proud to do in order to provide for his family – his young son Bain and his two daughters: little Tilda and Sigrid. There is something intangible about Bard that makes him stand out from the other inhabitants of Lake-town, a certain nobility in his bearing, a quiet pride; and a rare integrity in a town that is corrupt to its bones. People look to Bard, moved by his natural leadership qualities.

Perhaps it is a pride in his ancestry that marks him out: for Bard is directly descended from Girion, the last King of Dale. Girion was killed when Smaug attacked the city, but his wife escaped to Esgaroth, and the family has lived there ever since. The Black Arrow is the last heirloom of Bard's family.

THE BLACK ARROW

Bound to a rafter in a poorly furnished room in an unprepossessing house in the run-down trading post of Lake-town, lies the greatest hope in the world of Men. It is not much to look at – a long black shaft, more like a lance than an arrow – but it is the last of its kind. Brought out of Dale by the last desperate survivors of the dragon's attack, it has been hidden away for many years; hidden and forgotten, by all but a few. It was made in the days of power and plenty, when the lords of Dale ruled a thriving realm. Once, as the legend goes, arrows like these were fired at the dragon Smaug by Girion, Lord of Dale, fitted into a dwarven-made windlance, the only weapon powerful enough to bring down a dragon. Girion failed to bring down Smaug, though it is said his last shot dislodged a single scale.

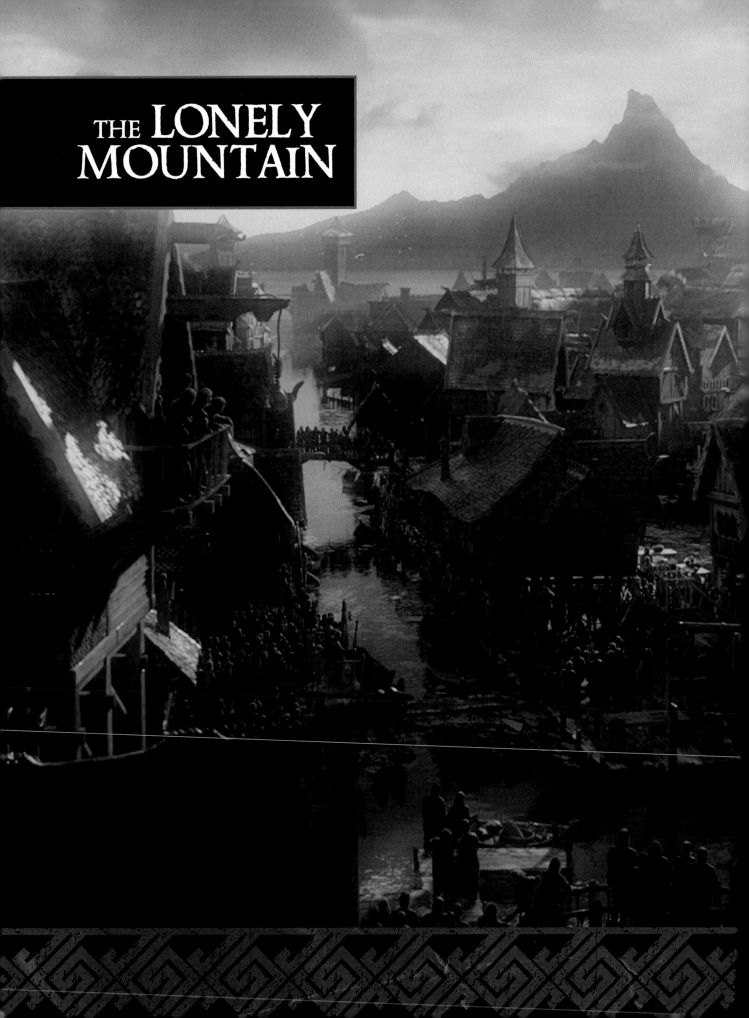

THE LONELY MOUNTAIN

In the north of the region of Middle-earth known as Rhovanion lies a solitary peak, hundreds of miles from any other mountain range. This is the aptly named Lonely Mountain, once containing the great dwarven kingdom of Erebor, home to the clan of Durin and the huge treasure they had amassed, until the dragon Smaug drove them out.

Just to the west of the Lonely Mountain is the great forest now known as Mirkwood because of the evil that has begun to corrupt it, and houses the realm of the Woodland Elves, ruled over by Thranduil. In a valley in its southern foothills, between two prominent spurs, lies the abandoned city of Dale, once a thriving, elegant and prosperous city of Men, and just below that is the Long Lake and the trading post of Lake-town.

To the north of the mountain lies the vast desolate plateau of the Northern Wastelands, once the breeding ground of dragons. The wasteland is bound to the north by the jagged Grey Mountains and to the west by the Misty Mountains, highest of which is Mount Gundabad, an Orc stronghold.

Beyond Gundabad lies Angmar, that chilly realm founded by a lieutenant of the Dark Lord in ages past, a base from which raids could be launched to ravage the kingdoms of Men. And if that evil realm was to rise again, then the elven strongholds of Rivendell and Lórien, and even the Shire itself might fall. The Lonely Mountain therefore occupies a highly strategic position.

EREBOR

Inside the mountain lies the ancient dwarven kingdom of Erebor. It was once the fortress-city of Thrór, most powerful of all the Dwarf-lords and grandfather to Thorin Oakenshield, who is now heir to his mantle as King Under the Mountain. The kingdom was built deep into the mountain and its beauty was legendary, with its soaring vaults and labyrinthine tunnels. The Dwarves were unrivalled in their mining skills, and in the roots of Erebor they unearthed precious gems – emeralds and diamonds, sapphires and rubies – and great seams of gold that ran like rivers through the rock.

At the last, they delved so deep they came upon the most extraordinary jewel of all: the Heart of the Mountain. The Arkenstone: a great milky white stone which glowed with incredible radiance. The Dwarves then used all their skill to work the gem into hundreds of shining facets so that when light struck it, ten thousand sparks of radiance would shoot from it, glittering with every colour of the spectrum.

Thrór saw the stone as a sign that he was destined to rule the kingdom of Erebor by divine right and he named it the King's Jewel: from that day it became the symbol of the rightful King Under the Mountain. And so for Thorin it represents far more than just a gemstone, for without it his claim rings hollow: it is crucial that of all the glittering treasures in the horde, the Arkenstone is the one object he must have and hold.

THE KINGDOM WAS
BUILT DEEP INTO THE
MOUNTAIN AND ITS
BEAUTY WAS LEGENDARY

THE CORRUPTING POWER OF GOLD

...NOT UNDERESTIMATE THE ... OF GOLD OVER WHICH A ...GON HAS BROODED.

Dragons are so powerfully associated with gold that the blind avarice for the yellow metal by any being – human, Dwarf or Elf – has come to be known as 'dragon sickness'.

Yet, where dragons are concerned, there is no logical explanation for the greed for this substance. It may – in some eyes – be beautiful to behold, its rich golden hue warm and brilliant, constant and untarnished. In the world of the free peoples of Middle-earth, it has long been regarded as precious, sufficiently prized as to be a valuable trading currency, able to render its possessor rich and powerful; What earthly use do dragons have for gold? They cannot eat it, cannot win influence or breeding partners with it; they cannot work it as the Dwarves do, nor do they need coin for trade: what a dragon wants it takes by fire and force.

It ensnares them as if its very nature is sorcerous. Once they scent gold, dragons cannot leave it be, but must do whatever they can to acquire it, to gather and hoard it. They will storm and burn the settlements of Men and Dwarves if gold calls to them from within, harrow and slaughter any who try to come between them and the treasure. Once they have taken possession of the gold, dragons will coil their bodies around and over it, even burrow into its depths, seeking the greatest possible surface contact with the precious stuff as if trying to draw sustenance, warmth or energy from it. And yet it is nothing but cold metal: it is not unknown for dragons to starve to death once they have established a hoard, they are so in love with their treasure, for they may refuse to stir from guarding it, being fearful that someone will discover and try to steal it.

The obsession that grips them is so unnatural it may as well be regarded as a malady: thus, dragon-sickness. And legend has it that the fierce covetousness a dragon feels for its hoard may even over time seep into the gold itself, ready to infect other greedy souls.

D warves are particularly susceptible to the malady of dragon-sickness. For them it becomes for them a dangerous form of love-sickness, whereby they can think of little beyond the object of their affections. This susceptibility appears to be innate to their race and may have a great deal to do with their affinity with the things of the deep earth – the ore and mithril and gems they have mined, the seams of gold that run like rivers through the rock on which their kingdoms are founded. Dwarves have mined for precious substances for millennia: they have a feel for detecting them and then for working the metals and jewels they have unearthed into beautiful and powerful objects.

King Thrór, Thorin Oakenshield's grandfather, was King Under the Mountain at the height of Erebor's greatness and the treasure he amassed during his reign sent him mad. Ironically, his success in hoarding gold was what attracted the attentions of the worst dragon of all: Smaug the Magnificent, who then attacked the kingdom and the city of Dale.

It is no wonder that Thorin Oakenshield is destined to succumb to dragon-sickness. It is in his blood, his inescapable heritage. For almost two centuries (for Dwarves are very long-lived) Thorin has dwelled on the loss of the Kingdom of Erebor, and especially the treasure of his father and grandfather, taken by the dragon. Too much thought of gold will corrupt even the most gentle soul, dreams of avarice that will become corrosive and poisonous, destroying all ease of mind and warping all logical, sensible perspective.

So much gold! So many jewels! And all infected by the brooding thoughts of the treacherous wyrm that had taken possession of it all these years. Before long, he forgets to eat, and cannot sleep.

As his trusted, but now ignored, counsellor Balin says, the new King Under the Mountain may sit on a throne with a crown on his head, but Thorin is less than he has ever been.

GOLD BEYOND
MEASURE, BEYOND
SORROW AND GRIEF

Elves may be the oldest of all the races of Middle-earth, immortal, ageless and ethereal but sometimes even the most ancient wisdom may give way to dragon-sickness.

King Thranduil of the Wood-elves has a great love of beautiful things. He has, in his palace on the edge of Mirkwood, created a place of great elegance and beauty, filled with glorious carvings and fabulous elven artistry. But sometimes a love of beauty can give into covetousness, even into obsession.

Centuries ago in the time of King Thrór and before the dragon's attack, Thranduil designed a beautiful necklace for his wife. He gave into Thrór's own hands the materials with which to make it, since the elves do not work metal themselves: the finest raw gold, silver and some superb jewels – famed far and wide as White Gems of Lasgalen. And with these materials, the dwarven smiths fashioned a wondrous work of art, a necklace fit for an elven queen.

But there was a dispute over payment for the work carried out and King Thrór refused to part with the necklace. Some say the necklace was so beautiful that he could not bear to let it go and so devised the complaint; others take the dwarven king's side and claim that the elven king short-changed him. Whatever the right of the matter, the dispute created a rift between these two noble peoples, and Thranduil's obsession with reclaiming the necklace burned so fiercely it distorted his good judgment, for in his mind it was the last thing he owned that reminded him of his dead wife. It is remarkable that so small a thing should create so great an obstacle between the alliance of the Dwarves and Elves against the forces of evil. And it is sad that in his obsession over the necklace, Thranduil should have forgotten a more tangible legacy of the love he and his wife shared, in the flesh-and-blood form of his son, Legolas.

Perhaps of all the peoples of Middle-earth, Men are the weakest and most susceptible to dragon-sickness. Greed for gold is ages old.

Easy to see how the Master of Lake-town fits this pattern. Between the idealised vision he has of the man he might have been – represented by the handsome self-portrait in his chambers, or the clean-cut golden figurehead on the prow of his barge, gazing bravely and blindly out at a world he has never travelled – and the man he has become there lies a huge gulf and immense tension.

Perhaps he once dreamt of greatness, but over the years power and easy money have corrupted him. Greed rules him – for food, for gold; but it is gold that has mastered the Master. But what can you spend your filthy lucre on in Lake-town? The place has gone to wrack and ruin: and now the gold has all but run out.

The greed for gold has shaped his life: now it will shape his demise.

Alfrid's fortunes are bound to the Master's: always he has trailed in the corrupt politician's footsteps. Twisted in body and soul by his craving for the power and influence his poor childhood denied him, he has bent every iota of will and intelligence on clawing his way up to the position he now holds: batman, pot-emptier, enforcer; lickspittle. Yet it is not a role he relishes. Gold represents for him a sniff at autonomy, a glimpse of power. But it also represents his downfall.

GOLD AND POWER
THE RINGS OF POWER

Three Rings for the Elven-kings under the sky,
Seven for the Dwarf-lords in their halls of stone,
Nine for Mortal Men doomed to die...

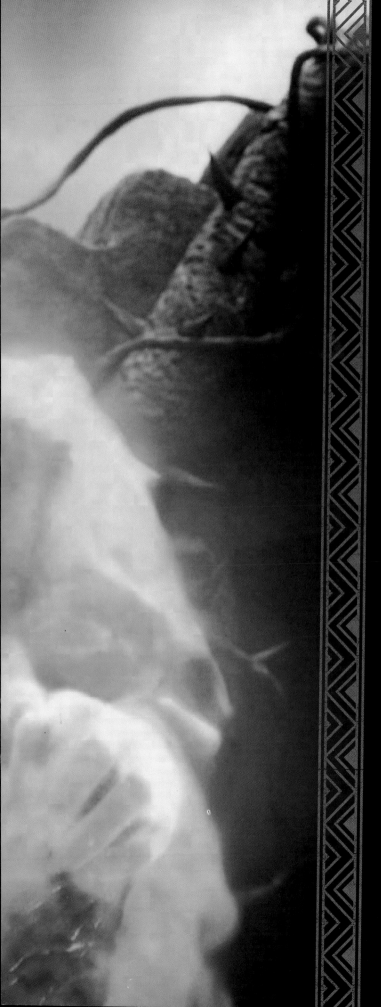

U p in the remote, wind-scoured
peaks of the High Fells of
Rhudaur nine tombs were sealed
with powerful magic, the occupants
interred there as far from the rest of the
world as it was possible to be. The inhabitants of these tombs were once kings of
Men. The Nine. But those tombs now lie
broken open and empty...

Once these kings were offered gifts by
a powerful lord: gold rings, ostensibly in
reward for their services. The rings came
with promises of power and immortality,
and the Nine were ensnared.

These gold rings were not simple
gifts, for the Dark Lord had forged them
to cast a spell over the wearers, drawing
them into his influence. In need of power
and substance himself, he had designed
the rings so that they would enable him
to leach the kings into himself, body
and soul, reducing them to wraiths.
Incorporeal, but imbued with his dark
magic, now they do his bidding, enslaved
by the rings they bear.

THE
TREACHERY
OF SAURON

One for the Dark Lord on his
dark throne,
In the Land of Mordor where
the Shadows lie.
One ring to rule them all, one
ring to find them,
One ring to bring them all and in
the darkness bind them
In the Land of Mordor where
the Shadows lie.

It was the Dark Lord Sauron who had ordered the Rings of Power forged, including the One Ring, the most powerful of all. By these treacherous means he attempted to bring under his control all the peoples of Middle-earth.

The kings of Men fell easily beneath his dominion; the seven Dwarf-lords, in thrall to the rings they were given, found themselves overtaken by greed for gold and were almost consumed by their own avarice. It is rumoured that Thrain, father of Thorin Oakenshield, wore one of these fabled rings. No one has seen Thrain since the aftermath of the Battle of Azanulbizarft

The Elven-kings, suddenly becoming aware of Sauron's masterplan, took off their rings and hid them from him until he was defeated in the great Battle of Dagorlad. It was there that Sauron lost the One Ring, for it was cut from his hand by Isildur who then lost it in a river, where it would be found much, much later by Gollum, the creature Bilbo Baggins encountered in the depths of the Misty Mountains. It is the One Ring that Bilbo now carries in his pocket.

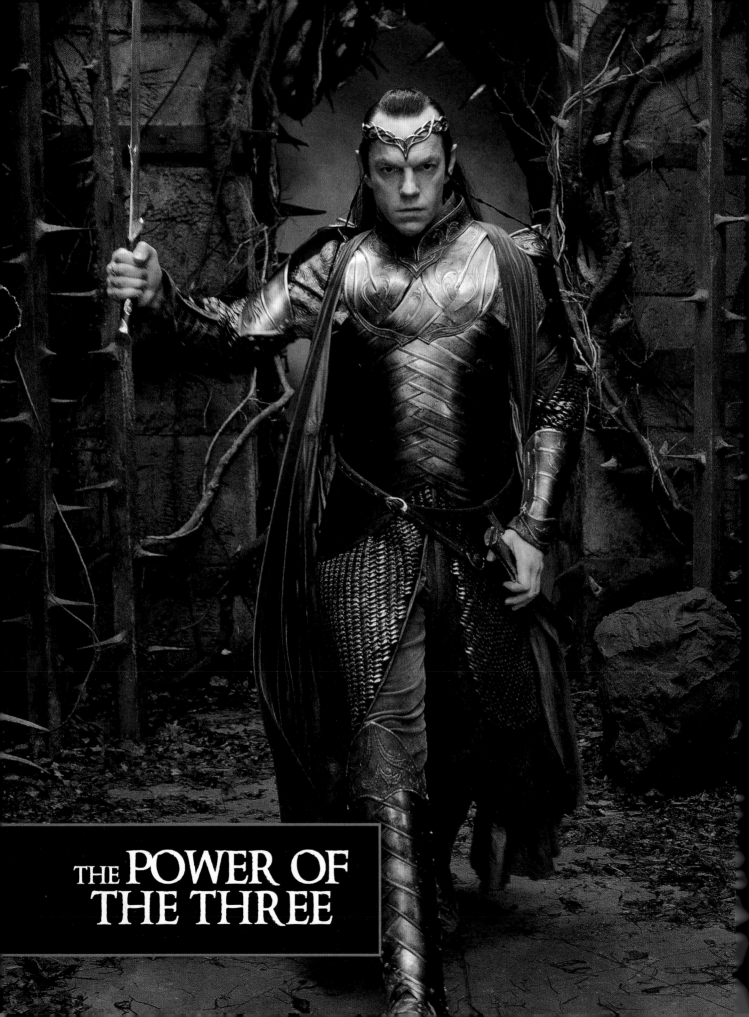

THE POWER OF THE THREE

The three rings of power held by the elves are in safe hands. Círdan the Shipwright, one of the most ancient and powerful of the Elf-lords, holds Narya, the Ring of Fire: he is far away in the West of Middle-earth, building ships at the Grey Havens.

But two of the most powerful elf-lords have faced Sauron's evil power before, and they are ready to do so again.

Galadriel, the White Lady of Lórien, called by the Orcs Zolta-grîshu, the Witch of the Wood, wears Nenya. The Ring of Water is made of that magical substance called mithril and is set with a white stone as bright as winter sunlight.

Vilya, the Ring of Air, created from gold and set with a bright blue sapphire, is the most powerful of the elven rings. It is worn by the Lord Elrond, Master of Rivendell. Long ago he served in the last alliance of elves and men to do battle with Sauron: and he will not hesitate to do so again.

THE ISTARI

Long ago, the Istari were sent to Middle-earth to act as guardians for the world: to gather knowledge, guide both elves and Men; and to combat evil. Although they go about disguised in human form – usually as elderly, if sprightly, wizards – the Istari are more than they seem, for they are Maiar, spirits whose being began before the world, and they have great and often hidden powers.

They are: Curunír, also known as Saruman the White; Mithrandir, called by most Gandalf the Grey, and Radagast the Brown, whose Maia name is Aiwendil.

Glamdring once belonged to King Turgon of the Noldorian Elves and represents the pinnacle of elven weapon-craft and bears an inscription in Elvish: 'Turgon, King of Gondolin wields, has and holds the sword Glamdring. Foe of Morgoth's realm, hammer to the Orcs'. It was lost after the Fall of Gondolin, A strengthening spell protects the user and it is so beautifully weighted that it can be wielded single-handed.

THE ISTARI ARE MORE THAN THEY SEEM, FOR THEY ARE MAIAR, SPIRITS WHOSE BEING BEGAN BEFORE THE WORLD

AN
ALLIANCE
AT **ODDS**

The time is upon us when all must choose which side they are on Evil is gathering, with the sole purpose of taking control of Middle-earth: now is the time for the forces opposing the creeping darkness to stand together. But there is division between those who should be in alliance.

There is a long-standing enmity between those two ancient races, the Dwarves and Elves, and when the great fire-drake Smaug attacked the dwarven kingdom of Erebor, King Thranduil and the elves of the Woodland Realm stood by and did not lend their aid and the Dwarves of the Lonely Mountain were massacred, their homeland burned and lost to them.

Elves, being immortal, have more to lose in war than any other beings in Middle-earth, but the Dwarves as a race have never forgiven what they regard as a deadly insult. And for their part, the Wood-elves consider the coming of the dragon as a direct result of the greed of King Thrór, since his heaped-up gold had attracted the monster in the first place. In addition there is the matter of the White Gems of Lasgalen, the jewels as white as starlight, that Thranduil is determined to regain and which the Dwarves swear he never paid for and will not release.

The Elves of Mirkwood are less wise and in some ways more dangerous than those of Lórien or Rivendell. Thranduil's instinct is to shut the doors to his kingdom and let the rest of the world get on with their wars; yet despite his great age and heritage, his power is fading and so is his empathy. All his thoughts turn inwards, and the corruption of the forest of Mirkwood finds a mirror image in its king.

Are we not part of this world? When did we let evil become stronger than us?

Yet there are other – younger – elves in the Woodland Realm who feel differently.

Legolas Greenleaf may well be his father's son, but his heart has not been corrupted nor has wariness become paranoia. In addition, his regard for Tauriel has opened his eyes to seeing the world in a different way, even if he – unlike her – has no love for Dwarves.

A TIME FOR HEROES

Some people – like the Master of Lake-town – have no time for heroes, considering them nothing but trouble and terrible role models. But then, some people care only for their own skins and do not want to see things shaken up. Heroes come from the most unlikely places, and in the most unlikely form.

From among the lowly and downtrodden, they will rise: not just those scions of the last Lord of Dale, like Bard and his son Bain, who must surely have the blood of heroes in their veins, but the women and children of Lake-town, armed with whatever they can scavenge or cobble together. For these people are not only fighting for a future, but for their very lives – and for a moment of pride in an existence that has afforded them till now neither dignity nor respect.

As members of the royal house of Durin, Thorin Oakenshield's nephews Fili and Kili have been raised on hero tales and songs of battle. They are young and reckless, too young to know the horror of war, too inexperienced to have seen their comrades fall or their people burn, as older members of the Company have. And they dearly wish to win the approval of their dour uncle and inspire hero-tales and battle-lays of their own. Perhaps, being of royal blood, they were born to be heroes, like Thorin himself. But perhaps that propensity places them in greater danger...

Of all the Company, one member is the least likely hero of all. It is one thing to be expected to be a hero and know you must live up to expectations. But it is quite another to have been brought up in a sheltered place where people lead quiet and simple lives and bravery is something other people in strange, lands possess. If, like Bilbo, you come from the Shire courage is not a quality regarded as necessary, or even laudable and to consider oneself a hero is to be getting above your station. Not that Bilbo regards himself as a hero. Not at all.

'Most of the time I was terrified,' he confides to Balin. 'But it never stopped you,' the wise old Dwarf replies: 'You kept going even though you were afraid, and that is true courage.'

In the course of his unexpected journey, Bilbo has encountered many dangers – perils he could never even have imagined back in the safe confines of his hobbit-hole on the Hill. He has faced trolls and gigantic spiders, Orcs and Wargs; even the wrath of a dragon, and never has he shied away or left his companions in the lurch. Quite the opposite, in fact: he has saved them not only by the quickness of his mind, but also by the quickness of his sword and a sheer indomitability of spirit absolutely remarkable in one so small or unsuited to the burdens of heroism.

TOO OFTEN THE COURAGE OF THOSE DEEMED THE LEAST OF US GOES UNMARKED

THE ELVES

It takes a great deal to persuade the Elves of Middle-earth to war. Immortal beings, they have the most to lose in conflict – a millennia of life and love and joy. But when they do fight, they are the most ruthless and efficient fighting force in Middle-earth. Though the dealing of death can never be beautiful to behold, when Elves wield their weapons it is with a terrifying grace more akin to dance than killing.

In the Battle of the Five Armies, the Elves must rise against the tide of evil that will otherwise encroach upon their realm.

The Elves of the Woodland Realm are highly militarized. Drilled and trained under the watchful, suspicious eye of their king, Thranduil, they are dark, grim and lethal. Their weaponry mimics the forest kingdom they have made their home: armour that enfolds the body with the delicacy of leaves; arrows with heads as elegant and sharply-pointed as a poplar leaf.

HE IS ONE OF THE GREATEST
FIGHTERS IN MIDDLE EARTH,
A FEARSOME, LETHAL WARRIOR.

Their king, Thranduil, rides into battle mounted on a giant elk and armed with two great Elven swords, designed to be used double-handed but so beautifully weighted and balanced they can be wielded with a single hand. Mercurial, powerful and arrogant he has a kind of ethereal ruthlessness. He is one of the greatest fighters in Middle-earth, a fearsome, lethal warrior. Cool of head, with the grace of a hunting cat, he is a deadly opponent, combining a terrible will and focus with the power of his kind.

Legolas Greenleaf, son of King Thranduil, is Prince of the Mirkwood Elves. With his famed long bow, he is one of the finest marksmen in Middle-earth, lightning-fast and accurate. His bow has been carved from a single piece of yew, and engraved with a delicate tracery of gold leaves with a quiver to match. Inside this quiver he carries narrow, steel-tipped bodkins that will punch through the thickest armour.

He also carries a pair of lethal White Knives made of fine steel, etched and engraved with a scrollwork of vines and honed on the downward side for slashing, and to a sharp point for stabbing.

No enemy can withstand him: he is renowned as the finest warrior of his age.

Tauriel is head of King Thranduil's Woodland Guard, and the king regards her almost as a daughter. His son Legolas regards her with more warmth than he would a sister, but it appears to be unrequited.

Tauriel is a graceful and deadly killing machine, mesmerising to watch as she executes her moves with the precision of a dancer. She is lethal with her short bow and twin filigreed daggers. She moves with the deadly stealth of a cat and fights with speed and agility, calmly but with venom, taking on multiple enemies at once.

She has devoted her life to the vengeance of her parents, who were long ago killed by Orcs. Nothing would please her more than to expunge every Orc from Middle-earth, and to watch her fight you would think she was determined to carry out this quest single-handed.

THE KING UNDER THE MOUNTAIN

In the heart of the mountain Thorin and his Company have found ancient weapons that belonged to the Ereborian Dwarves of old, before the dragon attacked the kingdom and slaughtered Thorin's people. The Dwarven axes they discovered in the hoard were the traditional double-headed axe, and the more elegant Ereborian single-edged axe, as well as crescent-bladed; throwing axes and warhammers. One of these weapons in the hands of an experienced Dwarf-warrior is fearsome indeed.

Thorin arms himself with a fine broadsword. The rest of the Company can take their pick of the axes, tridents and warhammers, or choose the mining tools left behind in the flight from the mountain. There is armour, too: boiled leather hauberks, vambraces and greaves, all decorated with traditional dwarven designs.

Of all those about to engage in the epic conflict, Thorin Oakenshield has the most to lose. His entire existence has been dedicated to winning back his lost kingdom. The scenes of the tragedy of the Fall of Erebor are seared upon his mind: the dragonfire, the panic, the brave but doomed attempt to withstand the assault; the massacre; the flight; the loss of all that was held so dear. And in all the years of wandering, of the homelessness and shame, of mourning and displacement, all that has inspired him to continue has been the dream of regaining his lost throne. Now that the dragon has departed he is dangerously close to realizing that dream: but at one and the same time, he is perilously close to losing it forever.

And so he will arm himself as befits a king, and go forth to battle...

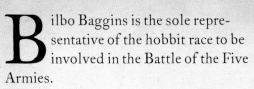

Bilbo Baggins is the sole representative of the hobbit race to be involved in the Battle of the Five Armies.

He is already armed with the blade that has earned the name he gave it when battling the giant spiders in Mirkwood Forest: Sting. It is an ancient blade of Gondolin, forged as a knife for a man of that legendary city before its fall. And one day that small sword – inscribed with Elvish script naming it as 'the spiders' bane' will come into the hands of another small hobbit – Bilbo Baggins' nephew Frodo – to be turned against an even more fearsome arachnid foe.

No hobbit was ever built to be any sort of warrior. Half the height of an Elf, half the breadth of a Dwarf, surely no armour in the ancient Ereborian hoard will fit a Halfling hobbit. But Bilbo is about to receive the greatest gift from a king that any warrior could be given: a mailshirt of pure mithril that Thorin has chosen for him from the ancient hoard.

In the Second Age, Dwarf miners hit a seam containing an unknown metal way down deep inside the mountain's roots. That seam turned out to be of mithril, a metallic substance said to be as light as feathers yet as hard as the scales of a dragon, and although it can be beaten like copper it can still turn the hardest blade. It is armour fit for a prince, fit for a hero; and Bilbo has already proved himself more than worthy of the gift.

SHIRKERS, INGRATES,
RABBLE ROUSERS!

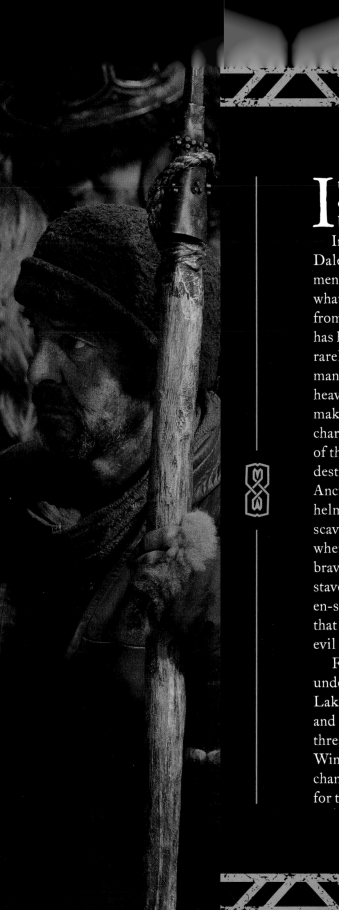

It is not only the Elves, Dwarves and one small hobbit who are readying for battle.

In the ruins of the once-great city of Dale, Bard the Bowman is inspiring the men and women of Lake-town to take up whatever arms they can glean or scavenge from the long-abandoned armoury. Bard has his trusty longbow, a weapon he has rarely had the opportunity to use these many years of serfdom in the Master's heavily-policed realm. But others must make use of what they can find amid the charred roof-beams and rotted timbers of the once-beautiful city the dragon destroyed in its fire-breathing rampage. Ancient skeletons will be stripped of helms and armour; swords and spears scavenged from amongst the cinders where the men who held them in their brave but hopeless defence fell. Sticks and staves, pokers and fence-posts, kitch-en-spits and butchery knives – anything that can be wielded against the hordes of evil that are converging upon Erebor.

For years these people have lived under the oppressive yoke of the corrupt Lake-town regime. Now they must stand and fight against a greater evil, one that threatens to engulf the entire region. Winning this battle represents their only chance to make a new and better future for themselves and their children

THE EAGLES

Always a law unto themselves, the Eagles are another formidable force in the world. They owe allegiance to no one other than Gwahir, the Lord of Eagles, and his fifteen chieftains. None other than Gwahir may command them, not even the Istari, though with Gandalf the Grey and Radagast the Brown they have a special understanding.

Eagles are not kindly birds, but when the future of Middle-earth lies in the balance, they can surely be counted on to weigh in on the side of light.

THE FORCES OF EVIL

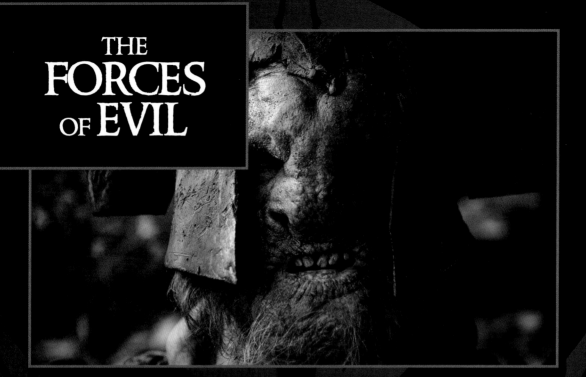

A huge army of Orcs is marching upon Erebor, monsters created in the dungeons of Angband and the cess-pits of Dol Guldur. Orcs are fierce and terrible warriors. They know no fear. But neither are they schooled or disciplined, just endlessly vicious and cruel, fuelled by an ever-burning hatred of all things that thrive in the light.

Orcs hate the sun. Some – like the goblins that infest the warrens of tunnels and caves beneath the Misty Mountains are quite terrified by it, living as they do in constant gloom.

The Misty Mountain Goblins are about the size of a Dwarf but far more feeble. But what they lack in individual power they more than make up for in numbers, for there are thousands upon thousands of them.

If they are to fight it must be under cover of darkness, and if not by night, then the darkness must be manufactured. Is this why clouds of bats have been seen swarming in northern skies?

The Giant Orcs, or ogres, come from Gundabad, the stronghold in the far north of the Misty Mountains. They are possessed of a great deal more vicious intelligence.

The commander of these legions is the giant albino Orc Azog the Defiler, who answers to the Dark Lord himself. He has a personal vendetta to settle amidst the wider conflict, for it was Thorin Oakenshield who cut off his arm at the Battle of Azanulbizar. As a result of this, he wears a prosthetic iron arm: and taking Thorin's head has become an obsession for him.

In turn, the King Under the Mountain has a score to settle with the giant white Orc, for it was Azog who took the head of Thorin's grandfather, Thrór.

A further huge force of Orcs is led by Bolg, spawn of Azog the Defiler. Amongst this horde are berserker Orcs which fight with a terrifying battle frenzy, annihilating everything in their path.

Many of the big Orcs are mounted on Wargs, those giant, vicious monsters bred from the wild wolves that once roamed throughout Wilderland. Wargs are not simple beasts, but have their own spark of cruel intelligence and even their own methods of communication – both with their Orc-riders, for they have a crude understanding of Black Speech, and with one another. They will often hunt in packs, and prey rarely eludes them, for they have keen eyes that can spot movement at a great distances by day or night, a remarkable sense of smell, and immense fangs and claws. Fast and powerful, they can run tirelessly.

They are not entirely trustworthy, even for those who ride them: many of their Orc riders are horribly mauled and scarred by unfortunate misunderstandings with their Warg-mounts. They barely feel pain and are hard to wound, for their hide is extremely tough and their skulls are like rock.

The forces of darkness also number among their army various different types of Troll.

Mountain Trolls, like those that Gandalf the Grey turned to stone after they captured the Company, are the most numerous. There are also Snow-trolls, Cave-trolls and the hardy Olog-hai. They are all huge, around twice the height of a man and many times his breadth, have immensely thick skins, tough skulls and are extremely strong. But they are also rather dim-witted, possessed only of great appetite and low cunning. They rely far more on their sense of smell than on their sight, for they have small, rather weak eyes.

When enraged (which is often) Trolls will attack whichever enemy is at hand, including their comrades, which makes them unreliable allies. They can be trained to carry out certain simple tasks, like hauling siege towers or battering rams, huge catapults or trebuchets. They are able to forge a path through the front rows of an enemy army by forming a mighty vanguard, in spiked helms and plate armour. Armed with long, spiked chains, maces and clubs, they are truly formidable opponents.

You have but one choice before you – how shall this day end?

And so at last the day has come when Light shall battle the forces of Darkness to prevent its vile shadow creeping over Middle-earth.

Battling for peace and restoration are the ancient indomitable race of Dwarves – of Thorin Oakenshield's Company and from the Iron Hills; the Elves; the men and women of Lake-town, and the Eagles. These are the forces of Light.

Opposing them are the vast horde of Darkness: beneath a canopy of vampire bats, the Orcs and Goblins, Wargs and Trolls. All of them answer to the one who came back to the world under the name of the Necromancer. Now he has revealed his true identity: the Dark Lord Sauron has come back to the world, desperately seeking dominion. If his armies prevail, the Free Peoples of Middle-earth will be doomed and his shadow will fall far and wide.

DREAMS OF HOPE

No battle ever truly ends in victory: there is too much to mourn, too many wounded, too many dead, too many evil sights seen, too many nightmares to haunt the sleep of those who have survived. But there are tiny seeds of hope that may be rescued from amidst the ruin and carnage and nurtured till they blossom.

For the surviving Dwarves, the Kingdom of Erebor lies awaiting the enthronement of its king and the remaking of its fame. The treasure is there in the great halls, spread as thick and golden as the fallen leaves in a beech forest in autumn; enough coin and gems to enable the long-lost homeland to be rebuilt to its former glory, for old and new debts to be paid and the pride and self-respect of the ancient, noble race to be restored.

And for the people of Lake-town, which lies now in smouldering ruin, there is a new dream of a future. Girion's great city of Dale was once a beautiful, fortunate place, full of villas and parks, pillared arcades, elegant bridges, ornamental lakes, and luscious gardens full of flowers and vine-fruit. Its forges rang with the sound of hammer on anvil, its streets bustled with traffic and a thriving market occupied its central square. People lived a good life here. Here, their children were raised in comfort and security.

In Lake-town, it was impossible for anyone to dream of a better future. But now Bard, direct descendant of Lord Girion of Dale, will be able to allow himself to imagine the city restored and rebuilt, the old destruction cleared away, the ancient tragedy avenged. Once more the city may be full of life, full of hope.

The displaced people of Lake-town have great need of hope, of a promise of a new beginning under all the dirt and blood. And so Bilbo Baggins gives to them the acorn he took from Beorn's home. He was going to plant it in his garden at Bag End: but they need this promise of hope more than one small hobbit. Besides, Bilbo has another keepsake which will serve to remind him of all that has been experienced, all who have been lost, all that is to come. A small gold ring, hidden away in his pocket...

Preciousssss...

HarperCollins*Publishers*
77–85 Fulham Palace Road,
Hammersmith, London W6 8JB
www.tolkien.co.uk

Published by HarperCollins*Publishers* 2014
1

A catalogue record for this book
is available from the British Library

ISBN 978-0-00-754411-0

Printed and bound in China

At last we have reached the end of this epic road! I must thank many of my companions along the way: my agent Jonathan Lloyd, publisher David Brawn and editor Natasha Hughes, designer Ben Gardiner, cover designer Stuart Bache, Charles Light and Kathy Turtle for production, Eleanor Goymer, Elena Thompson and Caroline Crofts in the rights team, brand manager Laura Di Giuseppe and Ann Bissell in marketing and publicity; and my fellow author and friend, Brian Sibley. At Warner Bros., Victoria Selover, Melanie Swartz, Elaine Piechowski, Susannah Scott and Jill Benscoter and Jayne Trotman; and most importantly Peter Jackson, Fran Walsh, Philippa Boyens and all the filmmakers, cast and crew who have been involved in making these extraordinary movies